Dear Parent:

Congratulations! Your child is taking the first steps on an exciting journey. The destination? Independent reading!

STEP INTO READING® will help your child get there. The program offers five steps to reading success. Each step includes fun stories and colorful art. There are also Step into Reading Sticker Books, Step into Reading Math Readers, Step into Reading Write-In Readers, Step into Reading Phonics Readers, and Step into Reading Phonics First Steps! Boxed Sets—a complete literacy program with something for every child.

Learning to Read, Step by Step!

Ready to Read   Preschool–Kindergarten
• big type and easy words • rhyme and rhythm • picture clues
For children who know the alphabet and are eager to begin reading.

Reading with Help   Preschool–Grade 1
• basic vocabulary • short sentences • simple stories
For children who recognize familiar words and sound out new words with help.

Reading on Your Own   Grades 1–3
• engaging characters • easy-to-follow plots • popular topics
For children who are ready to read on their own.

Reading Paragraphs   Grades 2–3
• challenging vocabulary • short paragraphs • exciting stories
For newly independent readers who read simple sentences with confidence.

Ready for Chapters   Grades 2–4
• chapters • longer paragraphs • full-color art
For children who want to take the plunge into chapter books but still like colorful pictures.

STEP INTO READING® is designed to give every child a successful reading experience. The grade levels are only guides. Children can progress through the steps at their own speed, developing confidence in their reading, no matter what their grade.

Remember, a lifetime love of reading starts with a single step!

Copyright © 1985 Sesame Workshop.
All rights reserved under International and Pan-American Copyright Conventions.
Published in the United States by Random House Children's Books, a division of
Random House, Inc., New York, and simultaneously in Canada by Random House
of Canada Limited, Toronto, in conjunction with Sesame Workshop. Sesame Street,
Sesame Workshop, and their logos are trademarks and service marks of Sesame Workshop.

www.stepintoreading.com

Educators and librarians, for a variety of teaching tools, visit us at
www.randomhouse.com/teachers

Library of Congress Cataloging-in-Publication Data
Lerner, Sharon.
Big Bird says— : a game to read and play / by Sharon Lerner ; illustrated by Joe Mathieu.
p.   cm. — (Step into reading. A step 2 book)
SUMMARY: Sesame Street Muppet characters play a game in which they obey commands
from Big Bird.
ISBN 0-394-87499-4 (trade) — ISBN 0-394-97499-9 (lib. bdg.)
[1. Games—Fiction.   2. Stories in rhyme.]
I. Mathieu, Joseph, ill.   II. Title.   III. Series: Step into reading. Step 2 book.
PZ8.3.L5493 Bh   2003 [E]—dc21   2002013231

Printed in the United States of America   48 47 46 45 44

STEP INTO READING, RANDOM HOUSE, and the Random House colophon are registered
trademarks of Random House, Inc.

Big Bird Says...

**A Game to
Read and
Play**

by Sharon Lerner
illustrated by Joe Mathieu

Random House 🏠 New York

I know a game called
"Big Bird Says"
I'd like to play
with you.
Just follow me
and read along.
I'll tell you
what to do.

Big Bird says

to touch your nose.

Shut your eyes.

Then touch your toes.

Touch the top
of someone's head.

Touch someone
who is in bed.

Brush your teeth

and wash your face.

Put on your shoe

and tie your lace.

Big Bird says

to touch the floor.

Put on your coat.

Go out the door.

Pull a wagon.

Bounce a ball.

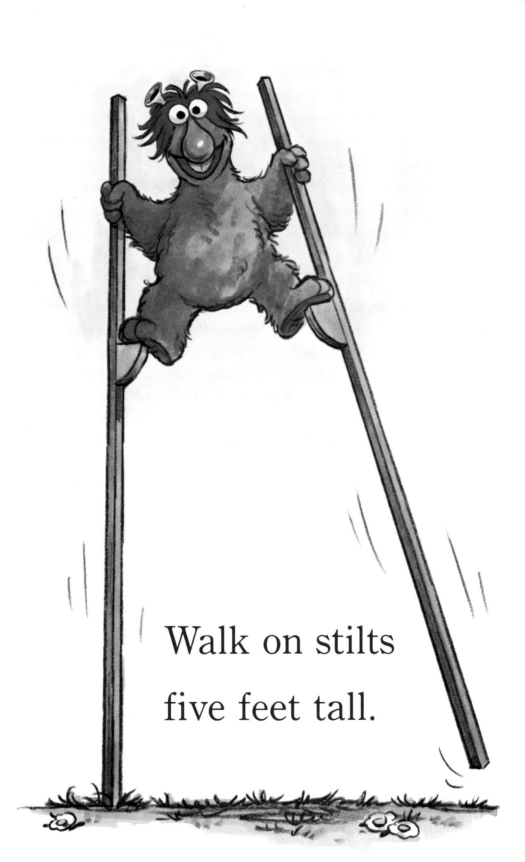

Walk on stilts
five feet tall.

Find a girl.

Then a boy

Share your very
favorite toy.

Big Bird says
to catch a goose.

Find someone
whose tooth is loose.

Find something
that makes you lucky.

Touch something

you think is yucchy.

Pat a dog.

Then pat a cat.

Kiss someone
who wears a hat.

Big Bird says
to say bow-wow.

Quack like a duck.

Moo like a cow.

Jump way up high
and flap your wing.

Stand on your head
and start to sing.

Draw a picture
of a clown.

Now do the same thing
upside down.

Touch your elbow.

Then your knee.

I'll tickle you.

You tickle me.

I'd love to play
some more with you,
but now YOU tell
ME what to do!